Illusion at Midnight

Ashley Bríon

Published by Ashley Bríon, 2022.

ILLUSION AT MIDNIGHT

First edition. May 31, 2022.

Written by Ashley Bríon.

Also by Ashley Bríon

Watch for more at https://www.slucas0.wixsite.com/authorashleybrion.

Andre watched in the shadows as the raven-haired woman walked along the artificially lit streets. After almost a century of searching, he found what he'd been looking for, and had been watching her for days.

It has to be her, he thought.

Back when they were young, she had beautiful golden hair that glittered under the sun, something he could never see again, but she looked just the same and as beautiful as ever. He could tell that she sensed his presence since she often stopped and looked around. She shivered against the growing cold sweeping over the clear September night. *Now,* he thought, *you have to say something!* But what could he say? Hi, I'm Andre, you probably don't remember me, my dear, but we were lovers hundreds of years ago, and I finally found your reincarnated soul?

No, he had to be more cunning than that.

On the first day he mustered the courage to make his presence known to her, he sent her a dozen lilies; her favorite flower. When she found them on the doorstep, she was taken aback, but picked them up, smiled, breathed in their fresh fragrant scent, and took them inside.

After watching her put a flower in her hair every day for a week, he sent her a note asking if they could meet in three days' time at midnight.

Today was that day.

Andre watched as she slowly strolled to the meeting spot, a small Victorian brick home, where he noticed she often spent her time writing, reading, and practicing spells all by candlelight. What he couldn't understand was why she had no memory of him. Why would she agree to meet someone she had never met?

As the two came close to their destination, he saw her start to become hesitant, looking behind her as though she wanted to turn back. *Please no,* he thought, *please, I must meet you, don't fret, my dear, you're safe.* As though she heard his pleas, her chest rose and fell with a deep breath, and she climbed the stone stairs to the house.

Andre stood on the other side of the street, hidden by a large hydrangea bush. He quickly peeked into the dimly lit window of the house to see her lighting candles and moving to sit down in her favorite red velvet chair, the one with plush cushions and ornately carved legs of vines and leaves encased in gold. She poured herself a glass of red wine and began to fiddle with a stone in her hand, her eyes closed as if she were meditating. *As your favorite writer once said, screw your courage to this sticking place.*

His long black cloak billowed behind him as the wind picked up, gliding across the road to the steps. If his heart was still able to beat, it would be going faster than lightning could strike. Gently, he knocked on the door and waited. He knew the myth about vampires not being able to enter homes without permission was bullocks, but this wasn't just any home. This was the home of a powerful witch.

"Come in," she called softly.

Andre felt himself shaking as he reached for the doorknob and slowly entered, breathing heavily. He walked through the foyer, his highly polished black shoes clacking against the cherry-stained wood floor. When he saw her, he drew in a quick breath. She was just as beautiful as ever. Even though her hair color was different, her facial features were still the same. Her skin was almost as pale as his, her dark haunting green eyes were illuminated by long black lashes and black eyeliner. She always loved darker makeup, but her clothes were a change. She wore a short dark purple dress with a slit that extended up her thigh, revealing a pale, smooth leg with a tattoo of some Japanese anime he couldn't place. Something to do with planets and princesses and a magical brooch. Sitting in the chair, she was looking away from him toward the roaring fireplace, twirling a tarot card in her hand: The High Priestess.

"They said I'd have a strange visitor..." she murmured, still looking away from him. The fire twirled and danced in her eyes. "But who exactly are you, and why have you been watching me?"

Andre was silent. How could he tell her he thought she was his reincarnated lost love? What woman would believe that? He wasn't used to this era of technology and odd romantic customs yet and wished this was as easy as it was when they first met in 1583.

"Well?" she demanded softly. "The cards said I'd have an unexpected visitor, but not *why* you're here. C'mon. Spill the tea."

Spill the tea? What on earth could she mean? Oh... one of those new 2000's colloquialisms. He had to say something, so he came up with an idea.

"Mademoiselle, if I may be so bold, I would like to invite you to have dinner with me."

She almost couldn't contain her laughter, pushing a fist to her mouth in an effort to stall it. How offensive.

"Do you really think I'd say yes to a total stranger who just waltzes into my life unexpectedly? You could be a vampire or a psycho for all I know!" She waved her hand in the air.

Andre felt his face pale even more than normal. Was that just a lucky guess?

"My lady," he started with a bow and a flourish, "I honestly did not think you would say yes, given as you don't even know my name. My apologies. My name is Andre Harcourt. I am from an old line of English nobles. I'm not quite used to American customs; please excuse me for my brash proposal."

She gazed at him, a curious grin flashing across her face. She studied him, reading his soul through his subtle movements. She stood and walked towards him. The heels of her black knee-high boots clicked across the floor until she was only inches away from him. Not taking her eyes from his, she bowed a low curtsy.

"My lord, I'd be delighted to have dinner with you."

Andre stared at her in shock. Why would she even agree to go to dinner with someone she only just met? And he didn't even know her name! This was turning out to be easy, yet a disaster at the same time. At least he knew what he was doing the last two times he found her...

"Lovely," he replied graciously. "May I pick you up Saturday at seven in the evening?" he paused, gesturing his hand toward her with a slight bow. "Where would you like to go?"

She appeared in thought for a moment, glancing at the ceiling then back down to the floor. When she looked up at Andre again, she boldly stated, "Would the Chateau de Brionde be alright?"

Andre let out a slight smirk. "That would be perfect. I'm sorry to have disturbed your evening and apologize for watching you. That was inappropriate of me. Do excuse my behavior."

The woman smiled and said, "You're excused. I have a lot of reading to do, so if you'll excuse me, I need to get to it."

"Oh... yes, yes. Please," Andre said quickly. He started to walk towards the door but turned as he approached it. "I can see myself out. Thank you. I will see you Saturday."

As Andre went to open the door, he heard her call for him. "Andre?"

"Yes?" he said, turning around back toward the parlour.

"It's Lily, by the way."

Lily? What was Lily? It was her favorite flower, the white ones that would glow in the moonlight and the tiger orange ones that were as fiery as her soul.

"I beg your pardon?"

"My name. My name is Lily Cordova."

"Thank you for the lovely evening, Miss Cordova." He turned and walked out the door.

Lily... he should've known her name would be something she deeply loved in her first life. As Andre walked down the street, he pondered why Lily was so willing to go out to dinner with him. This time it didn't make sense. The last three times he tried courting her in her previous reincarnations it took much more effort to get her to agree, but this time it was a simple yes after days of going about it the wrong way. He had an uneasy feeling, maybe it wasn't his beloved Victoria. He could have gotten the signals wrong, and this woman could turn out to be a madwoman.

A little late for such thoughts now.

As he walked down the street toward his colonial-style brick home on the other side of town, the light bearing down on him from the waxing crescent moon, Andre smiled. Saturday couldn't come soon enough.

THE TOWN OF MALO WAS small, with a population under 2,000, an old city built in the early 1600s by French immigrants looking to start a new life of prosperity in the New World. Andre had started to grow to love the old town, as it reminded him of his home in the countryside of England. If the courtship went according to plan, maybe this time they would stay here instead of taking Victoria home to England. *Lily,* he reminded himself, *her name is Lily now.*

The sun was setting, and soon he would be able to leave the house to pick Lily up for their date. He sighed as he stared at the mirror, looking at his pale reflection and dark eyes staring back at him. He thought about how the old myths of vampirism were completely unfounded. He could see himself in a mirror, he was undead, and not a spirit without a body. Garlic didn't do a thing, except make his favorite dish of garlic clove chicken from when he was fully human. He looked at the sunset and was glad soon it would start to become night earlier and he would be able to be outside more often. The sunlight wouldn't kill him, but it sure burned and made his skin resemble a serious allergic reaction.

Andre looked back at the mirror and straightened his cravat over his white silk shirt, his fine black tailcoat snugly trailing down his back. He grabbed his red velvet-trimmed cape and draped it around his shoulders. For a vampire, he was incredibly handsome with slick black hair, a chiseled chest with broad shoulders, and dark black eyes that could peer deep into the gates of the human soul. As the sun slowly sank beneath the hills of honeysuckle bushes and vineyards behind his home, Andre made his way out the door. The town was so small no one need-ed a car to get around, but given the colder evening, he opted to pick Lily up in his new Lotus Evija. Being over five-hundred years old had its perks in the ability to acquire a vast amount of wealth.

He pulled out of the driveway and drove the five small blocks to her Victorian home. He made his way through the cobblestone streets lined with beautiful trees of ash, oak, and Japanese cherry blossoms. With stores lined up on the sidewalk, the town looked like a perfect setting for a Hallmark movie.

When he pulled up to Lily's house she was already waiting on the porch. Andre had to catch his breath, the sight of her was intoxicating, he couldn't take his eyes off her. Her hair was done in a messy bun with strands of hair flowing over her face. Her makeup was tasteful, light and elegant with dark purple lipstick, her haunting eyes accented by eyeshadow that matched the purple hues of dusk. Her long gown was short in the front and draped to her ankles in the back. A touch of glitter caught the moonbeams from the rising moon. Her open-toed stiletto heels accented her delicate ankles and revealed a short silver chain with crescent moons and pentacles dangling from it. As she started to walk down the stairs, Andre scrambled out of the car and ran to grab her hand.

"Please mademoiselle, let me." Andre gently grasped her soft, black, gloved hand and guided her down the stairs. Lily let out a slight smile and a quick glance toward him as he stopped and opened the car door, gesturing for her to enter.

"Your carriage awaits my lady."

Lily softly chuckled. "Andre, that's so cliché."

"Ah, but it made you laugh. Then my job is done." He said, gently closing the door and smiling as he looked into her eyes.

On the way to Château de Brionde, Lily was turned away from Andre, looking out of the window at the passing trees and shops of the main drag. The lights started to turn on at this point and the street shined like white lights on a Christmas tree.

"Vi...Miss Cordova, is there anything wrong?" Andre asked. He caught himself from almost calling her Victoria.

Lily looked back at him and smiled. "No, nothing's wrong. Just admiring the lights and saving conversation for dinner. I love looking at the fall lights and decor the little shops have, and the pumpkins they put out near the square by the fireplace. I should take you sometime. It's so peaceful."

"I would very much like that, Miss Cordova. I enjoy a roaring fireplace at night to stave off the chill of the Autumn air," he said.

"Please, Andre, there's no need to be so formal. I know this is our first date and everything but calling me 'Miss Cordova' isn't helping us get to know each other, it's like I'm talking to a hired chauffeur. Call me Lily," she said.

Andre quickly looked back at her as they came to one of the only stop lights in town.

"Very well then, Lily it is."

As they pulled up to the Château de Brionde, a uniformed valet resembling a member of Napoleon's army opened the passenger side door and extended his hand to help Lily out of the car. Andre opened his door and came around the front of the car, tossing the keys to the valet.

"If you so much as put a scratch on this one, Damon, I will personally drain every drop of blood from your body, is that understood?" Andre growled in Damon's ear.

"Yes Mr. Harcourt. I promise I won't back it into the concrete pillar this time," Damon whispered.

"Very good." Andre slipped a $100 bill into Damon's coat pocket. "A little incentive to take care of my baby this time."

"Yes, sir," Damon said as he gently eased himself into the Lotus.

Lily watched them with interest but couldn't hear what they were saying.

"What was that about Andre? Do you know him?" she asked as Andre walked up to her to take her arm.

"Oh, nothing important," he said. "I was just remarking to him about the controls. These newer British cars can be a bit confusing for an American sometimes if they've never driven one."

"Oh," she said a bit suspiciously. "Ok, then. Shall we?"

"We shall."

Arm-in-arm, they walked through the open French doors and up to the host stand. The maître d looked up from his chart on his table and smiled a wide grin.

"Mademoiselle Cordova, Monsieur Harcourt! Such a pleasure to see you both again!"

"Bonsoir Alexandre..." Andre greeted with a haughty air.

"Hi Alex..." Lily said at the same time as Andre greeted Alexandre. Lily gave Andre a bit of a confused look, then quickly changed her facial expression to greet Alexandre.

"I have my best table for you tonight, right by the fireplace near the windows," Alexandre said.

"Perfect, Alexandre, I couldn't ask for a better table," Andre said.

"Right this way, mademoiselle, monsieur." Alexandre said as he gestured toward the dimly lit dining room.

The table held a small lit candle in the center with a small bouquet of tiger lilies in a black vase next to it. It was situated near the lit fireplace, and the sound of the wood crackled and popped with the dancing flames as they sat down. The window overlooked the town, since the restaurant sat up on a hill overlooking Sumter and Main Streets. Lily could see the glittering lights of the shops and a small glow from the square's firepit being lit. Andre let out a mental laugh at how obsessed the town was with fire and fireplaces. As they glanced over the menu for their drink orders Lily couldn't help but stare at Andre. Andre felt her glare pierce through his menu. He looked over the top of it then set it down on the table.

"Lily, is something wrong? You're not looking at your menu."

"Oh," she said absent-mindedly. "No, I'm just curious as to how everyone knows you. I know you've only been in town a couple weeks, judging from when you started watching me, which will be a topic of discussion later, and yet everyone here acts like they've known you for years. Is there something you're not telling me?"

Andre had to think of a lie quickly; he couldn't tell her the truth that the owner, and the workers at the restaurant were all old friends, since they too were also vampires who have moved from place to place over the last few hundred years.

"Oh, no, your assessment is correct," Andre said. "However, I've known the valet and the maître d for many years. Alexandre and I went to university together and Damon's family is from England, so I've known him since he was a boy."

"Oh...well...that's interesting, given Damon has an American accent and not a British one," Lily mentioned casually as she picked up her menu.

"He moved to America at a young age so instead of a British accent he developed an American one." He said quickly.

"Well, that makes sense," Lily said without looking up from her menu. "I think I'll end up going with the Petrus. I've been saving up to try a glass."

At that moment, their waiter walked up to the table.

"May I take your drink orders, Mademoiselle *et* Monsieur?"

Before Lily could speak, Andre started talking to the waiter. "May we have a bottle of the Petrus s'il vous plaît? On ice if you please."

"Oui, Monsieur Harcourt," the waiter said as he walked away to retrieve the wine.

"Andre! No! I can't let you do that, that's insane!" Lily anguished.

"Why not? It's one of my favorites. I'm sure you'll enjoy it," he replied, puzzled.

"It's over a grand a bottle! Do you even have the money for that? I mean...it's *a grand* for one bottle of wine!"

"It's perfectly fine, Lily. I purchase this all the time. My family has had a vast amount of wealth from old money. I've only enhanced over the years with stocks, bonds, and opening a marketing company for authors."

"Are you sure?" she asked.

"I'm sure. Please enjoy yourself and order anything you like. Money is no object." Andre returned to his menu.

Gaining money in stocks and bonds wasn't exactly a lie, but the last part was. It was on his to-do list. Rather than saying he made his money from not only being an English noble and in the royal family's good graces for hundreds of years, he also invested in inventions and other ideas he knew would become popular after a few decades, like indoor plumbing.

After the waiter dropped off the wine and took their meal orders, Andre couldn't hold in his question anymore.

"Lily... may I be frank?" he said as he poured her a glass of wine.

"Frank? Oh, you mean blunt. Yeah, shoot," she blurted as she took a sip of the Petrus. "Oh, mah, gawd! This is so good! I'm gonna have to sip on this..."

"Well, I'll make sure to have some on hand when you're around. What I was going to ask was why did you agree to attend dinner with me so quickly? I know I went about making your acquaintance the wrong way, which again I apologize for, but to agree to go out with a perfect stranger?"

Maybe if he was honest with her, he could judge her reaction here and determine how she would react to the truth when it was time. Lily took another sip and her eyes bore into him.

"Your energy, actually. As a witch, I can feel energies and I'm starting to be in-tune with my past lives by trying past life regressions. I haven't been successful yet. I know it sounds stupid, but I felt as if I knew you all my life and I was safe with you. I was off put by your stalking, obviously, but I never felt as if I was in danger. I know, hard to believe, isn't it?" Lily's voice almost cracked in fear of judgement, and she looked away from Andre as she finished her sentence.

"No, it's not stupid at all. I understand. I can sense energy, too, which is why I was drawn to you. I felt as if I've known you just as long."

Lily leaned over the table. "You're not just saying that to make me feel better?"

Andre almost spit his wine back into the glass. "Of course not! I would never. I am a man of honesty and chivalry."

Lily smiled. "Thanks. That's nice to hear these days. Men my age either want a slave wife or just get their dick wet. Nobody wants true commitment anymore."

Andre was a bit taken aback by her brash tone. The Victoria he once knew, and her other reincarnations, were spitfires and outspoken. Her spirit was strong, but he wasn't quite used to the outspokenness of the 21st century. He found it quite refreshing, but it was still odd to hear and an interesting transition from the days of his youth in the sixteenth century.

The night went along smoothly. Over dinner they discussed religion, philosophy, politics, literature, and history. Their laughter could be heard throughout the restaurant. Over dessert with slices of mille-feuille, Alexandre walked up to their table.

"Excuse-moi, Monsieur, the owner would like to speak with you."

Andre put his hand up to his chest, stood, and bowed toward Lily. "Excuse me Lily, this won't be but a moment. He probably just wants to catch up briefly."

"That's fine," she said between bites of cake.

As Andre and Alexandre walked away from the table, out of ear shot Alexandre whispered to Andre, "Do you think she suspects anything?"

Andre looked back at Lily, happily munching on her custard cake.

"No, I don't think she does. Not what we are anyway, but she does suspect something is different."

Alexandre ushered Andre up the plush carpeted stairs and around a corner to a large oak door engraved *Management*. Alexandre softly knocked on the door. "Fortunato? Andre is here."

"Come in," a voice called.

Andre opened the door and outstretched his arms towards a man sitting behind a desk.

"Andre! Amico! It's been too long."

"Fortune, it's been a few days and only a couple months before that."

"So? I've missed you!" Fortunato said as he embraced Andre in a bear hug. "Sit, sit."

Andre sat down opposite of the desk.

"Well, do you think it's her?"

"It's certainly her. Only took almost eighty years to find her this time."

"*Dio*, her death during World War II made her spirit more difficult to find this time, eh? And the universe didn't help putting her on a different continent this time," Fortunato said, pouring them two glasses of wine.

"No, it didn't. I'm starting to believe they made it so difficult this time because this may be the last time."

"*Non!* You really think so?" Fortunato shrieked.

"I do. The uncursed only get thirteen chances my friend, while we're stuck with whichever one we were last on. Who knows how many times she was reincarnated before I met her? This is number five, and her soul seems to come back every century."

"What does that mean, then?" Fortunato said as he handed Andre the glass.

"It means we have two options. Either let her die and be one with the universe forever and never see her again until we find a way to die ourselves or turn her." Andre took a sip.

"Andre, no. She's been adamant about not turning her in every life, she's not going to change her mind."

"She'll have to make a choice once she knows the truth!" Andre yelled and slammed the glass back onto the table, spilling red wine onto the oak desk and soaking a few of Fortunato's papers. "I'm sorry, old friend," Andre apologized immediately, anger seeping quickly away. "It's just I can't bear to lose her forever. We didn't know until after she died this last time how many chances a soul gets to be on this Earth. Maybe she knew and never told me, then forgot as she does each time she's reborn. If we're truly meant to be, she'll have to make that choice."

Fortunato sighed. "I know. I understand. Olivia made that choice when I found her again, and she barely questioned or even thought of the consequences of being cursed as we are. I felt that pain once of losing her, and I can only imagine the pain you must be going through, and the thought of losing her forever. She'll make the right choice, whatever she decides. Victoria was always a strong intelligent woman. Her soul will know what to do."

Andre smiled and walked around the table to embrace Fortunato again.

"Thank you, my brother. You've always looked out for me all these years."

"Someone had to, *mi amico*. Who else was going to teach you the ways of our cursed life? And stop you from killing every suitor that ever came near your dear Victoria."

Andre laughed. "I couldn't have asked for a better teacher. And I don't see that as a problem. Easy meals."

"Now go," Fortunato said chuckling, pushing Andre out of the office. "You have wooing to do, and you've kept that *bella donna* waiting too long."

"Demanding today, aren't we? You don't seem yourself. You never ask me to come into the office, you always come down the stairs. Afraid you'll get stuck behind a brick wall again with all that fancy wine you've been after?" Andre said mockingly.

"*Accidenti a te*, Andre! Don't start! That man Poe stole my name for his story after a night of drinking in that tavern when we visited New York! Now everyone thinks I'm named after that story! It's insulting!" Fortunato's flustered face burned red.

"Calm down, my friend, I was just trying to rouse your feathers, no need to get upset. I'll see you later." Andre said, laughing. He took his leave.

Andre was still getting over his fit of giggles as he reached the bottom of the stairs and headed toward the table. Lily had finished her cake and sipped her cup of coffee.

"Anything wrong?" Lily asked between sips.

"Oh, no, he just wanted to catch up on a few things and we got to talking about old times. Fortunato is a bit of a talker."

Lily snorted into her coffee. "Fortunato? Like Edgar Allan Poe's character from The Cask of Amontillado? Poor man having a name like that! His parents must have really loved that story."

It took everything in Andre's power not to burst out laughing. If his face could turn red, it would be like a tomato from how hard he was holding it in. He let out a loud cough and began to eat his *mille-feuille*.

After finishing the wine bottle and two more cups of coffee, they left the restaurant and headed toward the square under a blanket of stars. There wasn't a cloud in the sky, and the air was crisp and cool; a typical fall night in September. As they got out of the car, a few people greeted Lily and nodded at Andre.

Now he was in unfamiliar territory.

"C'mon," Lily gestured, "it'll be warmer over by the fire."

She picked a spot closest to the fire where a new wooden bench sat. They sat down and Lily began to rub her hands by the fire.

"I've always had a thing for fire. I love hearing it crackle, the smell of burning wood, especially oakwood. Something about it is so peaceful. Like an ASMR thing," Lily said softly.

Andre was barely listening; her voice was fading as it reached his ears. He was so busy staring at her beauty, watching the light of the flames play with shadows on her face. The light made her eyes shimmer.

"I'm sorry, I was lost in thought, what were you saying?"

"Oh, I was just saying about how much I love fire," Lily remarked without missing a beat.

"Ah, I do certainly love a good fire myself. I've worked around it most of my life and always found it soothing."

Andre almost mentioned watching the witch trials in Europe firsthand and remembered this wasn't Victoria yet, she still needed to regain her memory. And it may be a bit distasteful to mention witch trials around his now-reincarnated, witchcraft-practicing lover.

"What do you like to do Lily? Is this a typical day for you?"

"Drinking expensive wine at the most expensive restaurant in town and being picked up in a car my salary could never afford? No not really." She laughed. "I mostly work, and when I'm not working, I like to paint, or do those paint and sip things with friends. I practice my craft down at the meeting house where you first saw me, or I just take walks around downtown and shop or stay at home and binge watch my shows with ice cream and popcorn. I like to write poetry too."

Andre smirked. "That sounds lovely. I'd love to see your work sometime."

Lily peered at him, confused. "Work? You mean my paintings?"

"Both. Your paintings and your poetry. I adore poetry, and I love a good painting. I have a few Van Gogh's, a lovely piece by Picasso, and a couple of da Vinci and Raphael works hanging in my house. You should see the piece given to me by King Henry the Eighth."

As soon as he finished speaking, Andre knew he fucked up.

Lily's eyes grew wide with shock and disbelief. "King Henry the who? What do you mean gifted *by* him? He's been dead for centuries...?"

Andre had to think of a quick diversion. "Sorry. My apologies. I meant by his family. It's a portrait of him the Tudor family had handed down for centuries and one day it ended up in my possession through a series of art dealings."

"Oh! That makes more sense."

Good going, you bull's pizzle. You almost blew your cover.

They sat silently for a while, staring at the growing flames from the fire pit. The soft icicle lights lit up in the square and made the evening quite peaceful. Andre went over what Fortunato said in his head. He had to tell Lily sometime, and it needed to be soon. Otherwise, she would question why they couldn't go out during the day, his odd eating habits, and eventually why he wasn't growing old with her. During her previous incarnations her memory came back almost right away after they met, so he didn't have to face this conversation.

This time seemed different. Since she was silently staring at the fire, he replayed the events of her memory returning from her past lives. The first time she regained her memory she had come face to face with a mob of angry townsfolk on a witch hunt. As she was being tied to the stake, Andre calmed the crowd and convinced them she wasn't a witch before they lit the pyre.

The second time she regained her memory was during the middle of the Great War. Lily, then Marie, was stationed in France at a casualty clearing in Achiet-le-Grand. The casualty clearing site was subjected to a gas attack by the Austrians, causing Marie to breathe in toxic gas. Andre was a British soldier at the time being treated for a minor leg wound. During the attack, since being immortal he was immune to the gas, he carried her away from the gas, giving her his gas mask and performing CPR until she could breathe again. When she regained consciousness, she held him tight since her memory came back during her unconsciousness.

Then it hit him. *That's it! That's the secret! Her memory returns during traumatic events when she's faced with death!*

Now that he discovered the catalyst, he had to watch her every move. Who knows what this modern world would bring? Would it be a house fire? A car crash? A toilet seat falling from a plane in the sky? Who knew what it would be this time, but he had to make sure no harm would come to her.

"Andre? Are you alright?" Lily's voice yanked him back to the present.

"Hmm? Oh yes, just lost in thought. Old memories," he admitted.

"Did you want to go? You don't seem in the mood to talk anymore."

Andre's voice rose as he began to apologize. "No, no it's fine. I'm sorry I didn't mean to ruin our evening with my absentmindedness."

"Oh, I didn't mind it. I sometimes love silent company. It's nice to be able to sit with someone in silence and just take everything in. I was just hoping you were ok and if I did something wrong." She stirred the fire with a poker resting on the side of the pit.

"No, everything's fine, and you've done nothing wrong, my lady. I've thoroughly enjoyed our time together."

"You said you know a lot about British history, right?" Lily asked suddenly.

Andre was a bit taken aback. "Oh, well, yes I've studied every part of it." *And lived it,* he mused in his head.

"Would you mind telling me more about the usurpation of Richard the second by Henry the fifth? I'm fascinated about the timelines of the monarchy and always found Shakespeare's plays brilliant, but I feel they lack quite a bit of information. Just how do you switch dynasties so much when everything is bloodline-related?"

Andre's eyes lit up. When Lily was Victoria, she loved Shakespeare, and the couple were good friends of his. He was their favorite writer.

"I'd be glad to tell you."

After a long conversation about the British throne changing hands and how the monarchy worked for centuries, Lily realized the fire was close to dying, and no one else was around except a few police cars driving by or a stray person having a stroll. She quickly checked her phone.

"Oh gods! It's nearly three in the morning! We've been sitting here talking all night!"

Andre glanced down at his watch and found she was right. Soon he would have to get home before the sunrise.

"Would you like me to take you home now, Lily?"

"Unfortunately, yes. I need to get some sleep. I have a lot to do tomorrow with chores and baking. I promised my friend Callie I would have brunch with her and her fiancé to go over wedding plans," she rambled.

Andre stood. "That's quite alright. I need to be heading back myself for some sleep. I have a few errands to attend to tomorrow as well."

He held hand out to help her up. Lily graciously took it and kept hold of his hand as they walked back to the car. They laughed and giggled and talked as they made the drive back to Lily's home. She teased him about already knowing how to get there. After they pulled up to the curb, Andre was once again a gentleman, opening the car door for Lily and escorting her up the stairs to her door. Before she unlocked the door, she turned around to speak to him.

"Thank you, Andre. I had a wonderful time tonight. And I forgive you for stalking me."

Andre shook his head and let out a deep laugh. "You really aren't going to let me live that down, are you?"

"Nope." She giggled.

"Good night then, Lily." He bowed his head towards her and tipped his hat. Before he could turn around to walk back to his car, Lily grabbed him by the arm. "Is something..."

Before he could finish his sentence, Lily's lips were on his. He felt his emotions soar. He wrapped his arms around her and pulled her close. It felt like the first time he kissed her after he escorted her home from a wonderful banquet at the Queen's request after a day of jousting. The heavy scent of herbs and mead came back to him, only this time she tasted of expensive wine. Lily broke away to come up for air, biting her lip as she stared at him with need. Andre pulled her in and kissed her back fervently. All the memories came flooding back to him of each time he kissed her, no matter which reincarnation it was. He then broke free, trying not to let his tears spill from the emotions cascading inside him. He could tell she didn't want to leave him, and he waited to see if she would invite him inside.

Instead, she unlocked the door and opened it to step inside. "Good night, Andre. Thank you."

His mind racing, his unbeating heart somehow fluttering, all he could do was smile and say good night back as she shut the door behind her. Walking back to the car, he looked up at the second-floor window and saw her sitting by it, looking out at him. As he got in the driver's seat, he decided to place a call to Fortunato.

"My friend... I have some interesting news."

AS THE WEEKS WENT BY, and many dates later, Lily became closer to Andre. They would spend time at each other's home, take walks in the park, dine at their favorite restaurants, and sometimes drive to the beach a couple of miles away. She still hadn't regained her memory, but Fortunato and Andre's friends kept an eye on her when Andre couldn't, especially when Andre got an emergency call to head to New York for a couple of days concerning some stock business on Wall Street. Somedays he wished Alexander Hamilton never would have talked him into this stock market business when he visited New York City during Hamilton's time as the Secretary of the Treasury. He knew Fortunato would keep a close eye on her, but when he was dealing with business, he didn't have time to watch the news for about a week.

When he arrived home in Malo, he noticed all the windows were boarded up, and sandbags had been placed around homes and along the road. The gas station line was a mile long, and when he drove past the local grocery store, it looked as if a mob had picked it clean with people running in and out of the doors, their hands full of food, toilet paper, and batteries. Andre quickly changed lanes to head towards Château de Brionde. When he arrived at the restaurant, he noticed a sign on the door and the windows being boarded up by some of the employees, but he ran through the doors and up to Fortunato's office.

Fortunato looked up at his office door banging open as he stuffed papers and money inside of a large safe. When Fortunato saw Andre, he dropped the papers and sighed in relief.

"Oh, *grazie Dio* Andre, you made it home in time!"

"What the devil is going on, Fortune? The entire town looks deserted in a frenzy." Andre said as he gestured toward the window.

Fortunato started talking quickly as he began shoving more papers into the safe. "Don't worry *mi amico*, I already placed enough sandbags around your home, activated the emergency system, and boarded up the windows. You have enough blood to last you for a few months. I even added some raw meat from the kitchen to the emergency stores you have in the basement, which, by the way, we moved all of it to the top floor, and made sure the backup generator is working."

Andre grabbed Fortunato's shoulders and spoke slowly. "Fortune, slow down. What. Is. Happening?"

"There's a *uragano*, a hurricane, coming." Fortunato sighed. "It's bad. It formed quickly and strengthened to a category three, and it's expected to go out to sea and regain strength before hitting us. The town has never seen a hurricane like this before, it's unheard of. We may get lucky, and it will turn before it reaches us, but it's unlikely."

Andre collapsed into Fortunato's chair across from his desk. "My god..." He immediately thought of Lily. "How is Lily? Is she alright?"

Fortunato held his hands up. "Lily is *bene*. She seems scared, but her home is well prepared. I'd see if you can talk her into staying with you, otherwise if something happens, you won't be able to save her this time. It's not like the myth where we can turn into animals and fly wherever we want. And your speed won't help you over water and high winds."

Andre nodded his head. He knew that to keep Lily safe from this, he would have to force her to stay with him. But what would happen if she refused?

Fortunato broke him out of his thoughts. "Didn't you know about this, *mi amico?*"

"No, I didn't. I was so busy dealing with business I didn't have time to watch the news," Andre said softly.

Fortunato took his friend by the shoulders. "Go to her. *Subito*. We don't have much time. The hurricane is due to arrive in two days."

Andre didn't respond, but instead hurried out the office. He needed to get to Lily quickly and convince her to stay with him so he could keep her safe. Until her memory came back, he wouldn't be able to find out if this was her last life on Earth. Andre ran to his car and raced down the main street to turn onto Lafayette Lane toward Lily's house.

As he pulled up to the curb, her home looked deserted. Every window was boarded up with plywood and two-by-fours, sandbags lined the street and rows of them built a high fence up to her door. All her outdoor plants were gone, as were her lawn decorations. He climbed over the high wall of bags and pounded on the door.

"Lily! Lily, please let me in! It's Andre. It's very important! Please open the door!"

What felt like an eternity only lasted a few seconds. Andre could hear someone inside, and the thumping of feet down a flight of stairs. He then heard a voice coming from the other side of the door.

"Andre? Is that you? Hold on... I have to move some bags from in front of the door."

Andre heard the *thunk* and *thud* of shuffling sandbags for at least a minute, then the click of the lock on the door. Lily stood in the doorway with a wide smile on her face wearing a large crop-top sweater that stated, "Pumpkin Spice is Life Goals" and Sherpa-lined shorts with a pumpkin on the leg.

"Andre! You're home. I was worried about you," she gasped as she draped her arms around his neck.

"I'm perfectly fine, my dear. I was more worried about you when I found out."

She gestured for him to come in the door. "Come in, come in, quickly." As she closed the door behind him, she pushed a few sandbags out of the way. "As you can see, I'm perfectly fine. I have plenty of food and sandbags, all of the doors and windows, well except the front door, is boarded up and Jake the policeman is coming by later today with a few more supplies." She shrugged.

"That's exactly why I came to talk to you."

"Why, what's the matter?"

Andre regained his composure. "I'd like you to come stay with me during the hurricane. My home is set to withstand these types of events and I would feel better if you were by my side."

"Andre, this is my *home*," she said sternly. "I can't leave it. What about my cat? Giles must come with me. And my things? I can't just leave them. It's only a category three you act like it's the end of the world."

Andre could tell she was angry. "I'm sorry, I didn't mean it like that. We'll gather everything we can and put it in my car. I'll send some of my people over to get the rest and put what we can't haul into the attic. Giles is perfectly welcome to come, too."

At that moment, Giles, his black fur blending into the darkness on the floor, came around the corner and hissed at Andre before running into the next room.

Lily looked at Giles then back at Andre. "Giles! Stop that, it's not nice! Honestly I don't understand why he doesn't like you."

Damned cats sniffing out vampires from a mile away, he thought. Out loud he said, "Don't worry, Lily. He'll warm up eventually. It could be the cologne I wear, or I smell of something he doesn't like."

Lily glanced the house for what she needed to take. Most of the wall decor and easily moved, and furniture had been moved to the second floor, but the sofa, lounge chairs, and appliances remained in the living room and kitchen.

Lily frowned at Andre. "You promise me nothing will happen to my things?"

Andre wrapped his arms around her. "I can't guarantee that, Lily, I'm sorry. We can never know what exactly a hurricane will do, but I promise I do will everything in my power to keep them, and you, safe."

"Alright. I'll come with you. Let me grab some essentials and clothes and put Giles in his carrier and we can go."

Andre kissed her and nodded as he let her go and watched her walk up the stairs. While she packed, he placed a couple of phone calls.

"Emergency. Move everything you can of Lily, a.k.a. Victoria's, home to my home in Malo in twenty-four hours. Anything not moved in twenty-four hours, place it in the attic. I want sandbags around the attic, the doors, and the doors boarded up. The works against a hurricane up to a category five. Now."

As he hung up the phone from his last phone call, Lily came down the stairs with three large bags, a makeup bag, and an empty cat carrier. Andre quickly ran to take the bags from her.

"Here, my lady, I'll take those bags from you while you find Giles. Is there any food you need to take for him?"

"Yes, I have a large bag in the kitchen I haven't moved upstairs yet," she called as she went into the living room to find Giles.

Andre loaded Lily's bags and the bag of cat food into the car just as she came out the door with Giles in his carrier and holding a small bag of toys. "Ready!" she announced.

Andre closed the trunk and helped Lily into the car with Giles' crate resting on her lap. "Are you sure you're ok with this?" He said as he got into the car.

"Yeah, I'm all right. I think I'd rather be with someone during this than alone at home and something happen to me or Giles." Lily sighed as she reached a finger into Giles' carrier. Giles rubbed his furry cheek and whiskers on her finger.

The rest of the way back to Andre's home was silent except for Giles singing the song of his people. At the stop sign, Andre looked over at Lily and could tell she was scared. Her body was rigid, and she was shaking as she bit her nails. After they reached the house and Andre got all of Lily's things inside, he made her put Giles down so he could hug her tightly. He breathed in the scent of her jasmine hair.

"Don't worry. Everything will be fine. I've lived through a few hurricanes; we'll be perfectly fine here and we're well prepared."

"I hope you're right..." she trailed off as she looked at the sky through the one window on the first floor that wasn't boarded up yet.

In the next twenty-four hours, all of Lily's things were moved into Andre's home except her kitchen appliances. Lily saw some of her things being brought in during the day by some movers, but majority of her things arrived at night while she was asleep. She didn't see Andre much until the evenings, like always. Every time she asked one of his housekeepers or attendants where he was during the day, they would always say, "He works hard during the day and doesn't wish to be disturbed." She wished maybe she could talk him into a breakfast date one day, but they had to worry about the hurricane first. Lily watched the news, tracking its movements going out to sea below them, but turning in the sea, and now it was headed directly at them. She spent her time sitting on the couch, watching silently with Giles curled up asleep in her lap.

The day finally came, and the hurricane slammed into the town. The roaring winds and rain increased overnight, and lightning flashed from the very small cracks Lily could see through the boarded-up windows. After the front door and basement were sandbagged, Andre blockaded off the downstairs, and made sure even Giles couldn't squeeze his way through any bars or small areas. There was a second kitchen upstairs on the third floor and the food was kept in the attic, so there was never any threat of a food shortage.

After a few hours, a crack and the sound of splintering wood, a deafening creaking, could be heard outside and the lights went out. After a few seconds, the generator kicked in and everything came back on. Today, Andre wasn't working or hiding from her during the day. He was busy making sure radios had fresh batteries, his assistants were safe, and finally, holding Lily close. With the sun gone, he had no fear of being out during the day.

Lily shook in his arms. "Andre..."

"Yes, dear?"

"I'm scared." Her voice cracked and even Giles was on edge in her lap, and it wasn't due to Andre's presence.

"It's going to be alright. We're perfectly safe. Everything is fine."

"I think I'll go to my room and perform a protection ritual. I'll feel better." Lily's voice was monotone, yet full of fear.

Andre looked at her as she stood up, carrying Giles in her arms.

"Would you like me to go with you?" he asked.

"No, that's alright. I have to do these alone or I can't concentrate." She walked away from him and down the hallway to her room.

Andre watched her go, then continued to watch the news. The hurricane had quickly strengthened back to a category four right before it made landfall again. So far, the entire town was under at least eight inches of water, and the east end of town toward the sea was almost completely destroyed from flooding and a tornado that went through. Andre's home sat on a small hill on the north end of town, giving him an advantage to the storm. Or so he thought until he heard an odd sound coming from outside of the house. At first it sounded like a freight train, then he heard an odd moaning and groaning. The next thing he knew, he heard a horrible loud crunching noise, something crushing against the house as it shook the interior. Then he heard Lily screaming from the bedroom. With his quick speed thanks to his vampirism, he launched the door open. On the other side, there was no room. All he saw was a tree, water rushing below, and a pair of hands hanging onto what was left of the floor.

"Lily!" he screamed.

"Andre! Andre, please help me!"

Lily was handing onto dear life with one hand holding onto the rest of the third floor, and the other was cradling Giles.

"Take Giles first!"

Andre snatched Giles from her like a dragon hoarding money and quickly got him into the house. He belly-flopped onto his stomach to reach for Lily's hand.

"Lily! Lily, you have to give me your hand!"

Rain poured down on the both of them, soaking them to their core. Off in the distance, he could see a remnant of a path of a tornado, the funnel sucking itself back into the sky. Below Lily was a small fishing boat embedded into the first, and half of the second, floor of the house. If she let go, she would fall and impale herself on the broken mast. Andre reached for Lily, first grabbing her arm that was still holding onto the floor, and then reaching for her free hand. Her body was slippery, the rain making her slick and hard to grab.

Lily started to hyperventilate, her voice filled with panic. "Andre, don't let me go, please don't let me go..."

"No, no, Lily, I won't let you go. Just hold on. Reach up! I almost got you!"

As she reached up and he grabbed her hand, he began to pull her up and wrapped his arms around her waist. As he wrapped his arms around her, he missed her shirt, the wet skin-to-skin contact made him lose his grip, dropping her.

"*Andre!*" She shrieked. He watched as she fell, in slow motion. Her eyes were filled with terror, the sound of her screams reverberated off his bones, and his soul shattered. He had no choice; she would see what he truly was. He jumped from the floor, arching his body into a straight point, speeding through the air to reach her. As he grabbed her in mid-air, he twisted his body, so he landed on the deck of the boat, now being slightly moved by the rushing waters, and just missing the broken mast.

Lily landed safely on top of him. She clung to him tightly, looking up at him.

"Andre... how... how did you..." Before he could finish her sentence, her eyes changed from the dark green, to the turquoise blue they once were when she was Victoria.

"Lily, are you alright? Are you hurt?" he pleaded.

All she could do was smile, tears coming from her eyes as she said, "My body is alright. And I'd prefer you to call me Victoria, my lord."

Andre sucked in a sharp breath.

She remembers.

"Victoria... my Victoria! You remember!" He embraced her, kissing her passionately and deeply. His arms were so tightly wrapped around her she could barely breathe.

"I'm happy to see you too, darling." Lily, now Victoria, giggled. "Figures this would be the way I remember over five hundred years of lifetimes together—in the middle of a hurricane that was never meant to reach a town like this. Just like us."

"Who's the hurricane and who is the town?" He laughed. "Let's get out of here and back to safety inside the house."

As Andre helped Victoria up off the deck of the boat, they heard a loud creaking noise. They looked up to see part of the remaining floor in Victoria's room starting to collapse. The floor groaned, a bookcase, a large oak chest, and the bed started to come tumbling down onto them. Andre went to push Victoria out of the way, but she turned and pushed him instead. The bookcase fell into the boat and through the deck. The wood splintered in different directions, the force bouncing them away from the hole. Before Andre could grab Victoria's arm and move her away from the falling oak chest, the chest landed on top of her, sending both her and the chest through the deck of the boat.

"Victoria!" The sound Andre expelled was a twist between a dying man in extreme pain and a wild animal. He rolled over to the gaping hole and looked down, expecting to find the worst.

A soft, fleeting voice called up to him. "Andre... help ..."

Andre jumped down into the boat's cabin beneath the deck. Victoria was pinned under the oak chest. He could see her arm was broken, her leg was broken in two places, and the oak chest lay on her delicate chest, crushing her heart and lungs. Using his strength, he tossed the chest off her as if it was a piece of foam. He ripped her shirt open to reveal her chest. Andre could see that she had a few broken ribs and she started coughing up blood.

"No...no..." he cried. Tears streamed down his face. "Victoria, no, you can't."

He cradled her body in his lap as she continued to cough blood and tried to scream in agony. "Victoria... please you have to listen to me. We've had this conversation before."

Her eyes started to flutter shut as he took her face in his hands.

"Victoria! No! Please my love, we found out something new from the last time you passed! You only get so many lives, and we don't know which life you're on or if this is the last one! Please you must tell me if you want me to turn you! Please! If this is your last life, I'll lose you forever!" He could see Victoria slowly slipping away.

She reached for his hand. "Andre..." She coughed through the blood.

"I know it's a horrible, cursed life, my love." He continued. "I know. I know you'll never see the sun again; I know how we'll keep changing towns when people start getting suspicious, but we'll be together. I don't know if I can lose you again."

"Andre." She coughed again, stopping his rambling.

"Yes, my love?" He leaned down to listen closely, her hand gripping his as much as she could.

"Do it," she whispered.

For a second, Andre was in shock. All these years, through every reincarnation, she refused to let him turn her. It was as if she wanted to experience was death was like, knowing she would be back. He didn't know if she now knew this would be her last life, which prompted her to change her mind, but he was running out of time. Breaking out of his trance, he didn't hesitate to pull her up, hold her close, and kiss her, licking the blood off her lips before trailing down her throat to sink his now-protruding teeth deep into her neck. He felt her body stiffen and start to writhe in pain more than she already was.

He paused, her agony a knife twisting in his undead heart. "I know darling, I know. I'm sorry. It's going to be painful, but I promise it will be over soon."

Andre continued to sink his teeth in her, licking and sucking the blood from her neck, a trail of blood sliding down her shoulder, then across her breasts. Her warm body started to turn colder. Her once sun-kissed skin began to fade into a winter snow. The coughing and gurgles turned into horrific screams. As he slid his teeth out, he watched her face. He held her hand as he watched Victoria's eyes turn from terror and pain, to finally happy and free.

"I'm sorry, my love. I regrettably had to turn you, please forgive me..." he whispered.

"Forgive you?" she mused groggily. "For what? I asked you to turn me, you did nothing wrong. Could we please go back inside now? I'm a bit hungry and tired, and I'm sure poor Giles is terrified."

Andre was happy to lead the way, taking her in his arms and parkoured up the boat, onto the mast, and finally launch themselves up to the third floor where her room once stood.

"So how long do you think we'll stay here until we have to move?" she asked as Andre opened the bedroom door to re-enter the house.

"Well, it depends. Fortunato's been here for almost hundred years now and he uses the ruse of being the original owner's son then grandson. Somehow it works."

"Fortunato? Oh, my, Fortunato. I remember! We'll have to help him rebuild the restaurant after the storm. I don't know how long I can do without his delicious wine selection."

Andre pulled her into his chest, his mouth going down on hers and kissing her until her body melted into his.

"Don't worry, love. We have plenty of time. Would you like to read one of William's plays by candlelight as we wait out the storm, just like old times?"

"I thought you'd never ask," she cooed as she nuzzled into his chest, and he carried her back to the living room in the middle of the house. Giles padded behind them, looking curiously at his owner, and wondering why she smelled differently.

End.

Don't miss out!

Visit the website below and you can sign up to receive emails whenever Ashley Bríon publishes a new book. There's no charge and no obligation.

https://books2read.com/r/B-A-CVQP-UBNYB

BOOKS 2 READ

Connecting independent readers to independent writers.

Did you love *Illusion at Midnight*? Then you should read *Birth of the Wicked*[1] by Ashley Brion!

In her search for vengeance, Valerie finds more than she is hoping for, but what's a little revenge without sacrifice?

Valerie is tired of being a punching bag, enduring the cruel jokes and maltreatment from everyone around her, everyone besides Cordelia. Just when she's finally had enough, two girls invite her into their world and show her the power that they can wield. This dark magick is everything Valerie needs to enact her revenge, and her two new friends are more than willing to help her for a price.

---

1. https://books2read.com/u/bPgzEA

2. https://books2read.com/u/bPgzEA

Cordelia knows there's more beneath the surface, things that they aren't telling Valerie. Her intuition screams at her to keep her best friend away from them, knowing the rumors say they are a part of a coven that deals in dark magick. Will Cordelia pull Valerie out of the darkness, or will they fall to the malevolent magick that surrounds them?

Follow Valerie and Cordelia on a path of self-destruction, discovery, and the trials of friendship over one Halloween weekend.

Read more at https://www.slucas0.wixsite.com/authorashleybrion.

About the Author

Ashley Bríon is a 2013, 2015, and 2019 BA, MA, and MFA graduate in English and Creative Writing. Ashley has a long history of French and English heritage. She is bilingual speaking both French and English. She spends her free time gaming with her friends, acting, tap dancing, practicing yoga, and playing with her pets. Ashley embraces her love of history and different cultures through her writings, and is autistic and is a "social justice warrior" advocating for LGBTQIA+ and POC rights. Her favorite holidays are Halloween and Christmas and enjoys a cup of sake every evening.

Follow her on all her socials and sign up for her monthly newsletter on her website.

TikTok: @Jokergurl09

Facebook:

www.facebook.com/authorashleybrion

Instagram:

www.instagram.com/Jokergurl_cosplay_ashley_brion

Bookbub:

https://www.bookbub.com/authors/ashley-brion

Read more at https://www.slucas0.wixsite.com/authorashleybrion.

Printed in Great Britain
by Amazon

43203718R00030